Don't Forget Tiggs!

*Also by Michael Rosen
and illustrated by Tony Ross:*

Burping Bertha
Fluff the Farting Fish
Choosing Crumble

Don't Forget Tiggs!

MICHAEL ROSEN

ILLUSTRATED BY TONY ROSS

Andersen Press
London

First published in 2015 by
Andersen Press Limited
20 Vauxhall Bridge Road
London SW1V 2SA
www.andersenpress.co.uk

2 4 6 8 10 9 7 5 3

British Library Cataloguing in Publication Data available.

ISBN 978 1 78344 269 0

Printed and bound in Great Britain
by Clays Ltd, St Ives plc

Chapter One

Mr and Mrs Hurry were in a hurry.

They were always in a hurry but this morning they were in even more of a hurry. It was the hurriest hurry there has ever been.

They were hurrying by the fridge.

They were hurrying by the bathroom.

They were hurrying everywhere.

3

Then, in the most hurriest hurry of all,
first Mrs Hurry hurried out of the house
and off to work . . .

Whoosh!

And then, Mr Hurry. Off he hurried. Out
of the house, down the road, off to work.

Well, at least they had got everything done, so off they hurried with smiles on their faces.

good!

One problem.

Mr and Mrs Hurry had a son. His name was Harry. Or Hurry Harry as he was called at school.

And what had happened this morning is that Mr and Mrs Hurry were in such a hurry that they had hurried out of the house without Harry Hurry.

Either Mr Hurry or Mrs Hurry would usually take Harry to school.

But this morning, Mr Hurry thought that Mrs Hurry was taking Harry.

Mrs Hurry thought that Mr Hurry was taking Harry.

Mr Hurry and Mrs Hurry were too much
in a hurry even to say to each other,

This meant, in the end neither of them
took Harry to school.

oh dear.

So Harry sat in his room, on his own, wondering what to do.

He knew he was too small to go to school on his own.

He knew he was too small to stay at home on his own.

So, what to do?

Luckily, someone else lived with Mr and Mrs Hurry and Harry.

Tiggs.

Tiggs had seen Mrs Hurry leave.

Tiggs had seen Mr Hurry leave.

Tiggs had seen that Harry was on his own.

Tiggs thought about all this and then after a short while, he had an idea.

He ran upstairs, into the bathroom, then he leaped up on to the windowsill, squeezed himself through the window and jumped on to the top of the shed.

Harry looked up.

I know what that bervoom *is,* he thought.

That's Tiggs landing on the roof of the shed.

Then he'll jump off the shed and sit in the sunny bit in the garden.

Chapter Two

Outside, Tiggs did jump off the shed.

Harry was right.

But he didn't go and sit in the sunny bit in the garden. He jumped on to the wall and on to the pavement.

Then he bundled himself up into a tight ball of fur on legs and hurtled down the road.

He was running after Mr Hurry. He could smell Mr Hurry's aftershave and was following the whiff. Then up in front he could see Mr Hurry. He was standing at a bus stop.

The bus was just arriving.

Then as Tiggs rushed down the road towards Mr Hurry, Mr Hurry got ready to get on the bus.

But Tiggs knew what to do.

He ran faster and faster and got closer
and closer to Mr Hurry. And then he took
a huge jump and flew through the air
towards Mr Hurry.

WHEEEEEEEEE!

Just as Mr Hurry started to get on the bus, Tiggs landed on Mr Hurry's shoulder.

"Owwww!" yelled Mr Hurry. 'What's going on?"

"You've got a cat on your shoulder," said a woman helpfully.

"Oh, that's Tiggs," said Mr Hurry.

"Well, you didn't expect me to know his name, did you?" said the woman crossly.

Tiggs then got hold of Mr Hurry's ear and pulled it. He didn't pull it in any old ear-pulling way. He pulled it so that Mr Hurry had to turn around and face back home.

Mr Hurry stood puzzled and amazed.

"If you're getting on, get on," said the bus driver. 'If you're not getting on, don't get on," he added.

The bus driver was as helpful as the cross woman.

Tiggs couldn't speak English but he miaowed what he thought sounded like, "Home!"

Actually, it sounded like, "Miaow!"

Even so, Mr Hurry was getting the picture. He turned to the bus driver. "Tiggs wants me to go home."

"You can go where you like, pal," said the driver. "But if you're going by bus, stay on. If it's not by bus, get off."

"No, it's not by bus," said Mr Hurry. "It's by legs."

And with Tiggs now in his arms, Mr Hurry walked back home.

I wonder what this is all about, thought Mr Hurry.

Tiggs jumped down and led the way.

At the front door, Tiggs scratched. As soon as Mr Hurry opened it, Tiggs rushed upstairs to find Harry.

Harry was still there. He hadn't moved much because he was thinking about the wallpaper. He was wondering about the pictures of the birds and the crocodiles on the bit of the wallpaper by his bed. They were a bit wrong. The birds had the heads of crocodiles and the crocodiles had the tails of birds.

I think I know why that is, Harry thought. *Mum and Dad were in such a hurry when they were putting up the wallpaper, they didn't notice that it was wrong.*

Then in came Tiggs, followed by Mr Hurry.

"Harry!" shouted Mr Hurry.

"That's me," said Harry helpfully.

Seems like nearly everyone was being helpful this morning.

"You're not at school," said Mr Hurry.

"That's right," said Harry, "I'm here."

"Yes," said Mr Hurry, "you are."

"And you're wearing your trousers," said Mr Hurry.

"And so are you," said Harry to Mr Hurry.

"Why aren't you at school?" said Mr Hurry.

Harry thought about that for a bit, and then said, "Because you didn't take me."

Tiggs was thinking, *What is the matter with humans? Harry should be at school. Mr or Mrs Hurry should have taken him. They haven't. I've got Mr Hurry to come back but instead of taking him to school he's standing there talking rubbish.*

Mr Hurry seemed to realise this, and said, "Ah, right, you're right. You're so, so, so right, Harry! Let's go."

Then he hurried out the room and out the house with Harry.

Hmmm, thought Tiggs, *I'm not sure that Harry had any breakfast. Oh well, there'll be some food in school. I know about food at that school. I've seen it. Down Harry's school jacket when he comes home. He'll have some of that school-food at school, I'm sure.*

He paused for a moment.

Food...hmmm...hmmmmmmmmmm ...food...except...except...where is the food? Where is my food?

Shouldn't Mr and Mrs Hurry have left out his breakfast?

He went into the kitchen and over to his bowl . . . nothing in it.

Hey, this is a bit bad, he thought. *How am I supposed to get through the day without something to eat before they come back?*

Oh well, what's it to be, begging or raiding? Maybe a bit of both.

So, just like before, he went up into the bathroom, squeezed out through the window, on to the shed, and along the fence.

At first he tried a bit of begging.

He went up to a lady with a shopping trolley and said, "Excuse me, can I have some food?"

This came out as, "Miaow, miaow, miaow."

And the lady said, "What a lovely cat!"
And she stroked Tiggs.

Another human fool, thought Tiggs.
*I ask for food and they think that I want
to have my neck tickled. Duh!*

Just then he smelled something nice. The smell was coming from a bin. So he headed over to the bin and tried raiding it. He got on top of the bin. He clawed at it. He rubbed his nose on it. He jumped on it. He jumped on it again. It didn't work. All that happened was that he ended up dancing on the lid.

Not very good for getting food.

This sort of thing went on for most of the day until it was time for Mr and Mrs Hurry to hurry home.

Mr Hurry had remembered to pick up Harry.

That was good.

But it was Mrs Hurry's turn to do the shopping. And she had forgotten to do it. So, now everyone was very hungry.

Chapter Three

"I know," said Mr Hurry, "let's order some food from that cafe-shop-store website."

"Do you mean, All the Food You Want and More?"

"Yes, that's the one," said Mr Hurry.

So Mr and Mrs Hurry hurried to their computer and started ordering food from All the Food You Want and More.

Harry joined them to make sure that they ordered spaghetti. He loved spaghetti and he would be very unhappy if they forgot to order spaghetti.

"That'll do," said Mr Hurry. "Shall we get some spaghetti?"

And Mrs Hurry said, "No, not this time."

Then they did some more tapping on the keys and they got up and hurried off to do some important things.

Tiggs watched.

Harry sat and thought for a bit. His parents didn't seem to be very good at remembering him today.

Then he went over to the computer, and brought up All the Food You Want and More.

He found the button that said, "Change your order".

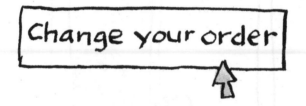

He found another button that said "Spaghetti".

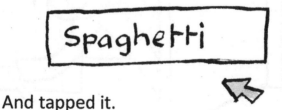

And tapped it.

A message came up saying, "You have ordered 'Spaghetti'. It will come with the chicken, rice, mixed vegetables and apple pie. It will arrive in 23 minutes."

"Wow," said Harry, and off he went to his room.

Then Tiggs leaped up on to the chair.

He put his paws up on to the keyboard and brought up All the Food You Want and More.

Tiggs found the button that said, "Change your order" and scrolled down the list until it got to "Cat food".

Tiggs looked at what was on offer.

It was so hard to choose.

In the end, Tiggs went for "GOBBLE!" because he thought it sounded just like the thing he did.

He clicked on "GOBBLE!"

A message came up, "You have ordered 'GOBBLE!'. It will arrive with the chicken, rice, mixed vegetables, apple pie and spaghetti in 11 and a half minutes."

Tiggs went off to sit by the front door.

Mr Hurry was hurrying through some knitting that he liked doing.

57

Mrs Hurry was hurrying through a crossword she liked doing. Well, she usually liked doing it but this evening the crossword was making her cross.

Then the doorbell rang.

It was the woman from All the Food You Want and More.

She handed over a box and they all gathered round the table as Mrs Hurry opened it up.

Out came the chicken and rice.

Out came the mixed vegetables and apple pie.

Out came the spaghetti.

"Did you order spaghetti?" said Mrs Hurry.

"Not me," said Mr Hurry.

"Hmm," said Mrs Hurry, "how mysterious."

Out came the tin of GOBBLE!

"Did you order GOBBLE!?" said Mrs Hurry.

"Not me," said Mr Hurry.

"Hmm," said Mrs Hurry, "how very, very mysterious."

"Chicken?" said Mr Hurry to Harry.

"Rice?" said Mr Hurry.

"Mixed vegetables?" said Mr Hurry.

"Apple pie?" said Mr Hurry.

"Is there anything that you would like?" said Mr Hurry.

"Spaghetti," said Harry.

"Sure," said Mr Hurry and gave Harry the spaghetti.

Then they all sat down to eat.

Tiggs waited.

He looked at the tin of GOBBLE!

Then everyone finished their dinner.

Harry and Mr Hurry and Mrs Hurry hurried about clearing the table and putting the dishes in the dishwasher and then they all hurried out of the room.

Tiggs looked at the tin of GOBBLE!. He
felt very hungry.

Chapter Four

Harry was in his room, thinking about what had happened today.

He remembered how he heard Mrs Hurry hurry off in the morning.

He remembered how he heard Mr Hurry hurry off in the morning.

He remembered how he sat in his room wondering about the birds and the crocodiles on the wallpaper.

Then he remembered the *bervoom* and thought about Tiggs landing on the shed and going off to sit in the sunny bit in the garden . . . But wait a minute . . . he hadn't actually seen Tiggs do that . . . he had just thought that that was what Tiggs did . . .

Harry went on thinking and figuring . . . figuring and thinking.

He remembered how Mr Hurry had come back to the house with Tiggs and taken him off to school.

Which was a good thing, he thought.

It wouldn't have been good sitting in his room all day . . .

Hang on a minute . . . does that mean, he asked himself, *that Tiggs jumped out the window, landed on the shed and then . . . and then . . . went and got Dad, because he knew I was left at home?*

Wow, he thought.

That's amazing.

Then he thought some more.
He thought about the spaghetti.
Nice.

Then he thought about something else that came out of the food box from All the Food You Want and More.

GOBBLE!

How come there was a tin of GOBBLE! in the box?

And then another picture came into his mind of Tiggs sitting on the floor looking at the tin of GOBBLE!

Oh no, thought Harry. *Kind old Tiggs, who rushed up the road to fetch Dad so that I could go to school, kind old Tiggs, who had to wait to order himself some GOBBLE!, is sitting downstairs without any dinner!*

Oh no, he can't open the tin himself.

So, Harry got up, rushed downstairs, and, sure enough, there was kind old Tiggs still staring at the tin of GOBBLE!

"Don't worry, Tiggs," said Harry, "I'll sort this."

And Harry picked up the tin of GOBBLE!, went over to the new Open-x machine that Mr and Mrs Hurry bought at All the Machines You Want and More and put the tin of GOBBLE! into the Open-x.

The machine went *DZZZZZ! KERCHING!*

Harry fetched a bowl that said "TIGGS" on it.

(That was why Tiggs was called Tiggs. When Mr and Mrs Hurry got Tiggs from All the Pets You Want and More and brought him home, they had a bowl marked "TIGGS" which they had bought from a shop called All the Plates You Want and More. So they named Tiggs after the bowl.)

Then Harry tipped the GOBBLE! into the bowl marked "TIGGS".

Tiggs said, "This is just great. Really great. It's worked out really, really well." But it sounded like, "Purrrrrrrrrrrrrrrrrrrrrrrrrrrr!"

So Harry stroked Tiggs which Tiggs thought was the first good stroke he had had all day. All the other strokes had been really, really annoying because they had come instead of food. Now this stroke came as well as food.

What could be better?

Good old Tiggs, thought Harry.

Good old Harry, thought Tiggs.

Just then, Mr and Mrs Hurry walked in.

"I just said that," said Mr Hurry.

"Me too," said Mrs Hurry.

"We would like to talk to you," said Mr
Hurry.

"You already are," said Harry.

"First of all, we'd like to say sorry," said Mrs Hurry.

"Sorry," said Mr Hurry.

"Secondly," said Mrs Hurry, "we want to say that we won't do it again."

"Do what?" said Harry.

"Leave you behind in the morning."

"Oh that's good," said Harry. "How are you going to make sure you won't do that again?"

"Well," said Mr Hurry, "we're going to . . . er . . . the . . . well . . . erm . . ."

"Yes," said Mrs Hurry, "we'll . . . erm . . . yes . . . and the . . . er . . ."

"How about you don't hurry so much?" said Harry. "You know, slow down a bit?"

There was a long pause.

No one said anything.

Then Mr and Mrs Hurry looked at each other.

"You know," said Mrs Hurry, "that's a very good idea."

"It is," said Mr Hurry, "I'd say that's a very good idea."

"Actually, that's what I said," said Mrs Hurry.

"Me too," said Mr Hurry.

"And I think I'll say it's a good idea too," said Harry, "even though it is my idea."

Tiggs looked up.

Yes, he thought, *it IS a good idea*.

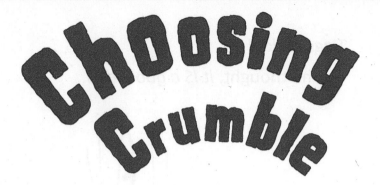

Choosing Crumble

BY MICHAEL ROSEN
ILLUSTRATED BY TONY ROSS

When Terri-Lee goes to the pet-shop she thinks she'll be choosing a dog – she doesn't expect the dog to be choosing her! But Crumble is no ordinary pet and he's got a few questions to ask:

How many walks will you take me on?
Do you like to dance?
Will you tickle me? I like that a lot.

Will Terri-Lee's dance moves and answers be enough to convince Crumble that she could be his owner?

9781849395281 £4.99